The Mystery of La Llorona and Mister Llorón

The Mystery of La Llorona and Mister Llorón
By Karen D. Gonzales

Copyright © 2024 by 303 Publications, Inc.

Published by
303 Publications, Inc.
Denver, Colorado

Paperback ISBN: 979-8-218-30255-9
Library of Congress Control Number: 2023919697

Cover and book design by Justin Kirscht and
Cover Lettering by Simon and Lyla Gonzales
Illustrated by Dolores Guerrero

First Edition

Printed in the United States of America

*My Llorona story for
everyone I know
and don't know!*

*Thanks to all readers of
this story,
especially those whose eyes,
ears or hands
helped to get it into a book.*

Happy Reading!

Contents

The Mystery of La Llorona and Mister Llorón

Meet

Darla Zapien

Jenel Chacón

Rolo Lucero

Joella Chacón

Jerred Chacón

Chapter One

Stars

A voice comes out of the dark.

"I've heard that if you count 300 stars, Lady Llorona will appear," Jerred says as he shines a bright flashlight in my face. "Darla, have you heard of Lady Llorona?"

Maybe Jerred thinks since I'm only going into the third grade, that I haven't heard of Lady Llorona. But I have. Hearing her name makes my heartbeat faster.

Jerred's the identical twin brother of Joella, my best friend Jenel Chacón's older sister. They are fifth graders and look alike, except Joella is taller with long hair. We're sitting on the grass in Jenel's backyard while our moms are visiting inside.

"Yes!" I blurt out. "I heard her crying one night at my cousins' farm in New Mexico. Lorena and Melinda said it was La Llorona. Do you think she's here in Colorado now?"

"Yeah," Jerred says as he sits on the grass beside us. "Let's count the stars and see. Two, four, six, eight..."

"Let's see who gets to 300 first," Joella says. She gets on her knees and points at the sky, counting quickly. "Six, seven, eight, nine, ten. . ."

I gaze up squinting but see only the half moon and a blur of fuzzy lights in the black sky. "I don't have my glasses on," I say. I'm scared that La Llorona might appear and I'm without my glasses. I don't like being the only one who has to wear them. And now with this short pixie haircut, I look like a boy and glasses look funny on me. My hair is as short as Jerred's now, but his looks like a porcupine.

"I'm not counting," Jenel says, pouting. "There's a billion stars up there. Besides, that's like calling her spirit here from New Mexico. That's too scary."

"Wait," Joella whispers. "I already counted 300. Look around."

"You probably counted the same stars twice," Jerred

says as he turns his head and looks around the yard. "We hear she's already arrived in our neighborhood. Sshhh, listen!"

Suddenly, there's a rustle in the bush by the fence. Jerred shines his flashlight at it. Two shining red dots appear, and out runs a big white cat from under the bush. It meows loudly, before jumping over the fence to the alley.

"¡Ay, chihuahua!" Jenel shouts. She hugs me. "Was that her?"

"No, it was just a white cat," I say. "Not a dog. But that scary meow kind of reminds me of the cry I heard at my cousins' farm."

Jerred says, "I never saw a white cat around here. That's strange for something white to jump out at us after Joella says she counted 300 stars."

Joella looks at her brother. "But you heard that the Lady Llorona can disguise herself," she says. "Maybe it was her and she was disguised as a white cat."

"I don't know whether to believe this," Jenel says. "Jerred and

Joella are trying to scare us. They always read books with scary stories. Darla, tell us about the cry you heard at your cousins' farm."

Chapter Two

Cousins

It happened at night last summer…

My cousins Melinda and Lorena and I were lying in bed and heard a strange cry through the window. It was really windy. The curtains were blowing around. Melinda jumped up and slammed the window shut. Then Lorena whispered, "Darla, that was La Llorona crying!"

I started shaking and was scared that someone was crying outside. "What does La Llorona mean?" I asked.

Melinda told me that La Llorona was Spanish for a crying lady. That she appears as a white ghost that haunts the arroyo near their farm. She cries because she can't find her child, who drowned.

La Llorona fell and hit her head on a rock while searching and drowned.

"What's the arroyo?" I asked. "Is that Spanish, too? That poor lady."

Lorena replied, "Yes, the arroyo is a creek that sometimes dries up, and when it has water, we hear La Llorona crying there. We don't dare go there at night because we fear La Llorona will get us. We hear she tries to steal children. There was this girl at school with bandages around her neck, and she said that when she was by the arroyo, La Llorona grabbed her by the neck. She got away with long scratches from La Llorona's bony fingers."

"Yikes," I tell Jenel. "I was so scared. I shivered and my teeth chattered like crazy."

"Oo-wee, that sounds scary," Jenel says in a hushed voice.

Chapter Three

Trance

"Is Lady Llorona here the same as La Llorona in New Mexico?" I ask.

"Yes," Jerred explains. "Her spirit wanders all the riverbanks from the country of Mexico all the way to Colorado. We just call her Lady Llorona here. She's the same white ghost crying at night because she either left her baby on the railroad tracks and the baby disappeared, or the baby drowned down the block in the gully—which is haunted."

"She will grab any kids that look Mexican, thinking they're her missing child. Kids with dark hair like you!" Joella says as she grabs my arm.

"Aaah," I say, whimpering and jumping away. It sounds scary, but I want to know more. "Where is she during the day?" I ask. "Does she disguise herself?"

"In the daylight," Joella says, "she disguises herself in different ways in the gully, so you won't recognize her."

Jerred adds, "If you stare at something down there too long, it could be Lady Llorona. If she sees that you've discovered her, she'll hypnotize you into a trance, and lure you to her. She's done that to people."

"Darla, we're leaving!" my mom calls out from inside the Chacón house.

Joella nudges me and says, "Don't dream about La Llorona tonight."

"Yikes, I hope I won't," I say. "See you tomorrow."

...

I get home and go to bed, peering out the window at the white half-moon. Then I think La Llorona might suddenly pop up outside my window. So, I get up and close the curtains and jump back under the sheets. When my brother Carlos comes back from the Navy I'll tell him  what I heard. I wish I had a sister about my age that I could share a room with right now. I say my prayers and hope to have nice dreams.

...

I go back to the Chacóns the next afternoon. The four of us sit on their front porch eating piñon nuts. I tell them about a weird dream I had last night of a girl walking around, but when I talked to her, she couldn't hear me. All of a sudden, Jerred and Joella point out a family coming down the sidewalk across the street. The mom and  dad are walking with their little boy and girl quietly staring as if they're in a daze.

Joella says, "Look at that Mexican family. They're in a trance, just looking straight ahead with their eyes wide open."

"Watch," whispers Jerred. "I bet they'll turn and go to the gully to meet Lady Llorona, when they get to the bottom of the hill and pass the railroad tracks. I bet she hypnotized them, and they're in a trance under her spell."

I watch as the family passes the tracks, turns, and walks right into the gully.

Jenel turns to me and whispers, "Oo-wee."

Chapter Four

New Friend

The next afternoon, Jenel and I play hopscotch on the sidewalk.

"BLAN-CA," someone calls. A Mexican girl about our age with curly black hair comes skipping towards us, turning her head to each side of the street while calling BLAN-CA over and over again. She's wearing a pretty black choker around her neck. As she gets closer, I can see a white cat face in a black heart on it, surrounded by another heart made of silver. She's taller than us and has big, emerald-green eyes. I think of the girl in my dream, who looked different.

"Hi, I'm Gloria Moralez," she says. "I just moved here. Have you seen a white cat running around?"

"Hi Gloria," Jenel says. "A white cat was in

my backyard the other night and jumped the fence and ran down the alley to the gully down the block probably. I'm glad to hear it may be yours. We thought she was this lady ghost."

"What kind of name is Blanca?" I ask. "That's a different name. Pretty velvet choker you have on. You also have pretty green eyes."

"Blanca is Spanish for white," Gloria explains. "I'm glad you like my choker and my eyes. What are your names and why would you think Blanca could be a lady ghost?"

"I'm Darla Zapien and this is Jenel Chacón," I say. "Well, Jenel's brother and sister said that this white ghost Lady Llorona might appear if we counted 300 stars. So, the other night after they counted 300 stars, a white cat jumped out of the bush. They also said Lady Llorona cries in the night down by the gully 'cause she's searching for her baby, who disappeared. Then she disguises herself in the day and can put you in a trance if you stare at something that could be her. She grabs Mexican kids, too."

Gloria says, "Nice to meet you. Blanca might be down in that gully then, because she's been missing for a few days. I should go down there to find her."

Jenel explains, "We never go down there because there are lots of tall, ugly weeds with stickers, big bushes, and skunks. The skunks walk up the alley in the night, and you can smell their stinky farts. And now we hear it's haunted."

"I sure don't want to get sprayed by a skunk," I say, shuddering. "One sprayed my neighbor's dogs and the smell stayed on them for weeks. I think there's quicksand near the gully, too. I've seen people on TV getting swallowed up when they step into it. Now Lady Llorona is down there, too. She might grab us and put us in a trance."

Gloria doesn't seem scared by what we tell her. She seems curious about exploring the gully to find Blanca and Lady Llorona.

"Let's see if we can find her and Blanca," she urges. "Besides, there are three of us. I think quicksand only exists in the movies, but we'll watch where we step and watch out for skunks. I don't want to go alone. Come on."

Jenel says, "Well, it might help us find out if what Jerred and Joella said was true. Since they aren't around, they won't know I went there. Want to go, Darla?"

"Okay," I say.

It's getting dark and cloudy. The wind picks up. Maybe a storm is coming. I'm a little scared, but don't want to show it, since Jenel doesn't seem scared anymore and we just made a new friend.

gully

The three of us go to the gully, veering away from the street and onto the old railroad tracks, searching for Lady Llorona in disguise. Gloria walks away from the tracks, then stops to stare at a dry, funny-shaped bush that's moving in the wind.

"Hey, maybe Blanca is in that bush," she says. "Blanca!"

Jenel asks, "Or what if that bush is Lady Llorona?"

"Don't stare at it, Gloria!" I shout. "Let's go back."

We start to walk away but turn back. The bush moves closer.

Jenel points and says, "Is that the same bush?"

"RUN!" I yell over my shoulder. "That has to be Lady Llorona. She's following us."

We run, leaving Gloria behind when she doesn't get as quick a start as us.

"Wait!" Gloria hollers.

Loud thunder rumbles.

Jenel and I both scream: "Aaah!"

Lightning flashes. Raindrops fall harder. The sky rumbles again. We're too scared to look back and don't stop running until we reach Jenel's house. We look at each other and realize that Gloria isn't with us.

"Where's Gloria?" I ask, wheezing to catch my breath.

"I don't know," Jenel says, shivering. "What if Lady Llorona stuck her bony hands out of the bush and grabbed her?"

Just then, we see Gloria turning from the tracks. She walks up the block slowly, staring into space with her big green eyes wide open, as if she's in a trance. Rain falls harder. Jenel and I wave to get her attention, but when she gets to the corner, she turns.

"Gloria, come over here!" I call out. But she keeps walking slowly, never turning to look at us.

"Do you think she's mad at us?" Jenel asks.

"Uh-oh," I say slowly, suspecting something awful. "Maybe Lady Llorona hypnotized her and she's in a trance."

Jenel turns to me with her mouth open, but she doesn't say 'oo-we' this time.

"This is so creepy," I say. I feel goosebumps all over.

...

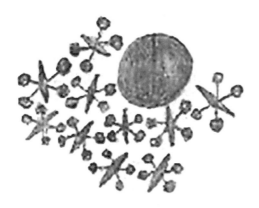

Jenel and I play jacks on my porch on the first clear day after a week of rain. All of a sudden, Gloria shows up. Her eyes are still open wide. We're happy to see her but watch as she comes closer to see if she's under Lady Llorona's spell. While we're figuring out a way to ask her about that day, Gloria confesses, "I was just fooling you since you didn't wait for me. I pretended to be in a trance like you said would happen. Let's go to the gully again."

I'm not sure whether to believe her story. Jenel has a puzzled look on her face. If Gloria wants us to go back to the gully, maybe it's to lure us to Lady Llorona. Maybe she really is under her spell.

"Did you find Blanca?" I ask, looking at her cat choker.

"Yeah, she came back that night," Gloria says.

I'm a little worried, but I look at Jenel and ask, "Do you want to go back to the gully again?"

Jenel nods and says, "Okay, but let's not leave

15

anyone behind this time. We have to come back up together. Let's try the other direction though, so we don't see that weird bush again."

"But that's the direction where the family in a trance went into the gully," I say. "What if we see them?"

Gloria smiles and says, "Maybe they're in disguise, too."

It all sounds creepy, but at least it isn't dark and rainy.

...

The three of us walk down the block to the railroad tracks and down a dirt hill to the gully. We stand around the edge, watching the water flow by while looking for Lady Llorona in disguise. I squint at the boulders with water rushing around them. That's when I spot the distinct shape of a face on one of the large rocks. It has eyes—one closed and one open—and a nose and green hair flowing around.

"IT'S LADY LLORONA!" I scream. "SHE'S A ROCK!"

In a panic, I turn and run up the hill. I slip on gravel and dirt and start to crawl, using my hands to pull myself forward. I can't get away fast enough. Someone pulls on my shirt. It has to be Lady Llorona grabbing me. I scream and pee my pants. But it's only Jenel trying to help. Gloria clamors behind us as we all try our hardest to get to the top of the hill.

"Where is she, Darla?" Gloria says, gasping as she stumbles to catch up.

"In the water," I say, panting. "She's disguised as a rock."

"How long did you stare at it?" Jenel asks, as if afraid I might be in a trance.

"Just until I saw her face and hair," I say out of breath. I might've stared too long, but I don't seem to be in a trance.

"Are you sure you could see a face without your glasses?" Jenel asks.

"Yes, I just can't see real far away. It had to be her."

The three of us reach the top of the dirt hill. This

time, none of us turns back to look at the creepy rock in the gully.

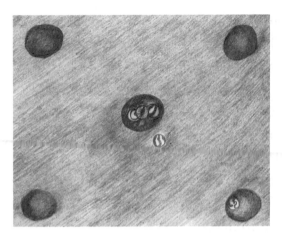

Chapter Six

Scolding

We leave the hill and run up the street where Jerred and Joella shoot marbles into five dirt holes in the ground outside their house. I tell them where we were and what I saw.

"Come on, let's go see if that rock is still there," Jerred says.

"No way," I say. "I'm not going back down there. We think we found Lady Llorona the other day, too, disguised as a bush because it started following us after Gloria stared at it."

"What?" Jerred says, scowling. "Jenel, you're not supposed to go to the gully. I thought you were at Darla's house. Why would you go down there?"

Jenel pouts and says, "Well, we met Gloria and

she just moved to the neighborhood and she wanted us to help her find her cat Blanca. But instead, we found Lady Llorona in disguise. I didn't believe what you said was true, but it is—she followed us."

Jerred gives Gloria a funny look. "Is your cat Blanca white?" he asks.

Gloria smiles and nods up and down, her black curly hair bouncing around. "Yes, Blanca means white in Spanish. She keeps sneaking out of our new house."

Jerred says to Jenel, "Well, if Lady Llorona was the bush, you could be under her spell and she's luring you back. Seriously, don't go to the gully again. Jenel and I never go down there. Mom and Dad will be really mad if they hear you went, and we'll all be in big trouble."

Joella says, "Okayyy… so you all promise not to go back. Because next time, Lady Llorona might grab you or put you in a trance and you'll disappear. The gully isn't a safe place to be walking around. Lady Llorona might start coming up here to find you!"

Jenel sighs and says, "Sorry. We'll promise not to go back if you don't tell our parents. We just wanted to help Gloria find her cat." She eyes her brother and sister nervously and fixes the barrettes that were sliding down from her wavy hair. "Why do you think she might come up here to find us now?"

Joella says, "Probably because she saw you all

snooping around and running away from her. She might even know where we live now!"

"Yeah," Jerred says, nodding. He lowers his voice and says, "And you're not going to believe this. Joella and I just heard scary news. Someone else just found Lady Llorona."

Gloria, Jenel, and I turn to one another and ask, "Who?"

Chapter Seven

Mister Llorón

"Mister Llorón," Jerred announces, "the father of their baby who disappeared. He finally found Lady Llorona down in the gully. They both drowned searching for their baby in different places a long time ago. So that's why their spirits are still wandering around rivers. Mister Llorón had been following Lady Llorona's cries along the rivers, hoping he could catch her and find his child that disappeared. He's been tracking her from Mexico for hundreds of years. This is the gully where he finally caught up with her—right down our block."

Joella adds, "So now, Mister Llorón is going to marry Lady Llorona. They will have a big Mexican wedding that everyone will be invited to. They'll get married in disguise as a couple that people will know. The wedding invitation will have the couple's name on it. Everyone will show up to the same wedding. They'll have a huge reception, and all the guests will watch and stare as they dance. And then they'll be hypnotized into a trance. They'll be under the spell of Lady Llorona and Mister Llorón."

It sounds pretty scary. I want to know more about this Mister Llorón and ask, "Does Mister Llorón also cry and search for the baby down by the gully? Is he also a white ghost at night and disguised during the day?"

Jerred says, "Yeah, he cries really loud and scary, too. That's why he has the name Llorón—the crying man. He's a tall, dark-gray ghost wearing a long coat and top hat. Half of his face is normal, but the other half is a skeleton. They were both seen floating around, dancing in circles. She looked like she was dancing with a real person, until they turned. Half his face was skeleton with glowing yellow eyes. Lady Llorona looked like a bride in a long, white wedding dress with a veil over a skeleton face, and her eyes were glowing red. I don't know if Mister Llorón disguises himself during the day, but he might since they're both going to disguise themselves as someone we know at this wedding."

Jerred pauses and nudges Joella with his elbow to have her continue. "Anyway," Joella says, "since they couldn't find their baby, they came up with a plan to have a wedding where families would gather and bring their children. They think that one of those kids could be their baby who disappeared years ago. After they hypnotize all their guests, they'll lure a child to go with them so they can be a family again."

Gloria looks doubtful. "Do they talk to people?" she asks. "Why would they tell someone about their plan? This sounds pretty weird to me. And it's hard to believe they can disguise themselves as people we know."

"Yeah," I say with a grin. "Well, if they're together dancing in circles and planning a wedding, they shouldn't be crying anymore, right?"

"Where did you hear all of this?" Jenel asks her brother and sister.

"I heard it from my friend Rolo Lucero, the boy in my class with two silver caps on his front teeth. He lives right next to the gully. His sister Rosa found out," Jerred says, "but we didn't ask questions. We need to be on the lookout for a wedding invitation, is all I can say."

Chapter Eight

Wedding Invitation

Jenel, Gloria, and I go back to my house to finish playing jacks on my porch and talk about the strange wedding. We plan to get the mail each day before our parents do, in case an invitation arrives. We talk about hiding it, so we don't have to go because it could be the wedding of Lady Llorona and Mister Llorón.

As we're making plans, Gloria asks, "Should we tell our parents or other people about this spooky wedding?"

"We better wait until an invitation comes," I suggest. "If we all get invitations with the same date and same location, then we should show our parents. We'll have to explain that something seems strange about getting invitations from people we know who will be getting married at the same place and time. Then maybe we can tell them what we heard."

Jenel says, "I'll probably show it to Jerred and Joella and let them decide what to do with it. They may not want to hide the invitation. Or maybe they will. Well, let's start playing jacks and see how many rounds Gloria can get to!"

"I've never played before," Gloria says.

"Really?" I say. "We can show you how to play and how to get to the next rounds."

...

Gloria comes over the next afternoon and shows us the wedding invitation she received in the mail. "My mom already opened it and threw the envelope away. She told me we'll be going to a friend's wedding next week."

"Oh no," I say. "Did you tell your mom about what we heard? We better write the address of the wedding down, in case we get one, so we can see if it's at the same place. That's sure a coincidence that we hear about a wedding and then one of us gets an invitation right away."

"Really!" Jenel exclaims. "Maybe you can pretend to get sick so you won't have to go, and your parents will stay home, too."

"Well, I didn't tell my mom what I heard yet," Gloria says. "If I pretend to be sick, they'll probably find a babysitter. Then they'll go and get hypnotized and not come back. But maybe it really is their friend's wedding and you all won't get an invitation. If both of you don't get one, I'll go because I like weddings, especially if they play music and dance. I love to dance!"

"Okay," I say, "just be careful and let us know if anything strange happens."

"Yeah, keep your eye on that bride and groom," Jenel says. "So, let's play jacks again. She empties the jacks out of 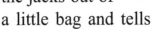 a little bag and tells Gloria to go first. Gloria touches another jack when picking up the onesies and fouls. I go next and get past onesies. On twosies, after I pick up eight jacks, only one is left when there should be a pair since there are ten jacks.

"I don't see the other jack," I say. "Is one missing or do I need my glasses?"

"Hmm," Gloria says with a moan. "Maybe it fell off the porch."

We search but don't find it.

Jenel seems upset and says, "I've never lost a jack before, that's strange! Well, we can finish playing with eight jacks, I guess."

We get all the way to Crack the Jack, Around the World, Pigs in a Pen, Cherries in a Basket, and no bouncy rounds. It's faster with only eight jacks. Jenel is a better player since she plays with Joella all the time. Gloria gets to the higher levels even though she hasn't played before. I should wear my glasses next time. It may help.

"Gloria," I ask, "where did you get that pretty choker and how come you always wear it?"

"It's my mom's," she says. "A friend gave it to her since she loves cats. But I like it because the cat looks like Blanca, so she lets me wear it."

"That's nice," I say. "Do you have sisters or brothers?"

Gloria shakes her head no and looks straight ahead. She doesn't blink. Her eyes are always open big it seems, but I don't want her to notice me looking at her for too long. I guess I shouldn't ask so many questions.

Chapter Nine

Wedding

Jenel and I watch the mail for wedding invitations, but nothing shows up. The day of the wedding that Gloria's family was invited to arrives and Gloria goes. All that day, we wonder if the wedding will be a normal one and can't wait to find out. A week goes by. Gloria doesn't come around. Jenel and I sit outside playing jacks, hoping she'll come by.

Jenel says, "She may have told her parents about Lady Llorona and Mister Llorón, and maybe they don't want her to play with us since we tell her strange things."

"Yeah, maybe," I say. "And we never asked her where she lives, so we can't even go to her house."

We decide to walk to the next block to look for her. We pass several houses she might live in, but no Gloria. We knock on some of the doors to see if she might open. But no one has seen a Mexican girl on the block. We haven't seen Blanca running around, either.

"Well, Gloria will probably go to our school," I assure Jenel. "We should see her there next week when classes start."

"What if it was the wedding of Lady Llorona and Mister Llorón," Jenel asks, looking concerned, "and Gloria and her family got hypnotized into a trance and never came back?"

"Whew," I sigh. "I'm sure glad we weren't invited to a wedding that same day, or we may have disappeared and be somewhere under their spell."

"Yeah, like down in the gully," Jenel says. "Gloria is probably fooling with us again to make us worry. She likes pranks, so let's just forget about her until she comes looking for us or we find her at school walking in a trance."

I giggle and say, "Yeah, with those big green eyes open wide. I don't think she ever blinked. Her eyes seemed to stay open all the time. And you know she'll be wearing her black velvet choker with the white cat on it."

"Really?" Jenel says. "Maybe that's why she was so good at jacks if she never blinked. Probably if she took the choker off, her head would fall off like that spooky story Jerred told us."

"Yikes," I say.

Chapter Ten

School

The summer of 1968 ends, and the four of us return to Coden School. My mom finally lets me walk to school with my friends instead of walking me herself. As we pass a house a few doors away, we see the neighbor lady standing at the screen door.

"Darla, do you know that big lady?" Jerred asks.

"Not really, but she's seems crazy and doesn't like us," I say. "Her name is Gretta and I think she is Jewish. These other neighbors are Jewish too, but they like us. She lives alone and always talks to herself real loud whether she's inside or outside. When my dad is outside, she tells him, 'Get outta here, go back to Mexico,' even though my parents are from New Mexico. My dad ignores her, but he always shovels her snow in the winter. My mom says we are Spanish, not Mexican, but I guess we look Mexican."

Jerred says, "Gee, how mean. I remember last Halloween when she gave us a handful of loose popcorn with brown spots on it. We just threw it away."

"I know," I say. "I hope no kids try to eat it. She does that every year."

...

We don't see Gloria in any classes at school to our surprise.

Jenel and I decide not to tell our classmates about the adventures we had finding Lady Llorona in disguise in the haunted neighborhood gully. We also don't mention our mysterious new friend, Gloria. And how she pretended to be hypnotized in a trance after staring at a bush that followed us. We also decide not to reveal the mystery about the wedding of Lady Llorona and Mister Llorón. Or how Gloria disappeared after attending their wedding with her family and we suspect they were hypnotized and put under a spell.

We think our classmates will probably tease us, especially the Jewish kids, unless some Mexican classmates heard about the Lady Llorona haunting the gully over the summer. So, we decide to keep it a secret. I wear my glasses in class since a few other girls wear theirs and I can see the chalkboard.

...

After school, we tell Jerred and Joella about Gloria going to a wedding and how we didn't see her again on the block or at school. They give us puzzled looks. As we walk home from school, Jerred points to an old, gray, two-story home on a corner that someone in his class said was haunted.

The side of the huge house is on 15th Avenue, and under the window is a sculpture of a sad-looking face that resembles the sun. The curtains in the window are old and torn and have a big, black stain on them, which Jerred says is dried blood.

The House with a Face...

Joella and Jerred tell us they have to go to school earlier tomorrow because they're taking band lessons to learn flute and drums. I can't wait until next year so I can take band lessons and learn to play the drums. Jenel and I will have to walk alone on Tuesday and Thursday mornings.

Chapter Eleven

House with a Face

Jenel and I avoid the sidewalk near the House with a Face as we walk to school on Tuesday morning. We walk on the sidewalk across the street playing Don't Step on a Crack or You'll Break Your Momma's Back. I peek over at the House with a Face when the curtains move. A girl's face appears at the window.

"L O O K — THERE'S GLORIA!" I squeal and point to the upper second floor window above the one with bloodstain on the curtains.

Jenel turns toward the house. "Where? I don't see her."

The girl disappears.

We wait to see if she'll come back to the window or to the porch. She doesn't.

"It was probably another girl, not Gloria," Jenel

snickers. Then she says with a tremble in her voice, "Darla, if that house is haunted, it may have been a ghost you saw."

"It sure looked like her 'cause her hair was black and curly all around, just like Gloria's. Maybe Gloria moved there. Should we go knock?" I ask.

"No, not now!" Jenel says. "I'd rather have Jerred and Joella go with us. The porch looks scary."

"Well, if she moved here, I wonder why she isn't going to our school," I ask. "What if she died and that was her ghost, like you said?"

"Oo-wee," Jenel says with a shiver. "Or maybe you just imagined seeing her. Plus, you aren't wearing your glasses again and that window is far away." She puts a hand on her hip and shakes her finger at me. "You better wear them."

...

Jerred and Joella walk with us on the way home. I tell them that I thought I saw Gloria in the window of the House with a Face that morning, but when Jenel turned she wasn't there.

When we arrive at the House with a Face, Jerred says, "Jenel, you and Darla go ring the doorbell and ask for Gloria if she doesn't answer. We'll walk you halfway to the porch."

Jenel pleads, "Not us. We're too scared. Will you and Joella go ask?"

Wooden floorboards creak as Jerred and Joella walk onto the steps. They reach for the doorbell, stop suddenly, and look at each other in a panic.

"AAAAAH!!!" they scream and race down and across the lawn.

"What happened?" Jenel says as she runs after them.

"What did you see?" I shout, running behind her.

They stop around the side of the house.

Joella says, panting, "There's a sign on the door. It  says, La Familia Llorones. This has to be the house of Lady Llorona and Mister Llorón. I bet when they got married, they hypnotized Gloria at the wedding, and she's living there under their spell. Just like we heard would happen. Why else would she disappear and then reappear in the window of a haunted house that says La Familia Llorones?"

We look at one another, bewildered. I look close at the sun face. It's right above, staring at us! Joella sees my mouth drop open and turns to look at the sun face. She starts pushing us forward, yelling, "HURRY! LET'S GET OUTTA HERE!"

"Wait up!" Jerred hollers. "Something is stuck

on the bottom of my shoe."

"Just run and wait 'til we get home to take it off," Joella says.

We run towards the sidewalk. I look back and can't believe what I see. The sad-looking sun face under the window is crying, a red tear like blood dripping from its eye. I'm so scared, I can't speak. My heart thumps harder.

I turn to my friends, who are ahead of me, and run across the two blocks to get to my house. I catch up to Jerred, who stops and lifts his foot. He pulls something out of the sole of his white Converse sneaker and sticks it in his pocket and catches up to us.

Chapter Twelve

Blue Cat-Eye Glasses

We get to my house and fall on the lawn to catch our breaths.

"Oh my gosh," I say with a moan. "You're not going to believe this, 'cause I can't either. You know that sad-looking sun face under the window? Well, I looked back, and it had a red tear like blood coming out of its eye. Then it rolled down its face."

"WHAT?" Jenel shrieks with her hands on her hips. "Darla, I think you're just imagining these things. How come we don't see what you see? I saw you looking back, but I didn't see a red tear on its face. Maybe you need to wear your glasses all the time, instead of just in the classroom where the other kids wear theirs."

"Um, okay!" I say, feeling dizzy. I reach into

my school bag and pull out my blue, cat-eye glasses decorated in gold glitter and put them on. "But I don't want to walk by and look at that old house anymore, even with them on. What if that sun face is her in disguise, if that's Lady Llorona's house?

If she's watching us walk by and we turn to look at it, she might hypnotize us and lure us inside."

"Wow," Jerred says, "check out what got stuck in my shoe when we were on the porch." He pulls a metal jack out of his pocket. "It was hurting the ball of my foot when I was running."

Jenel's eyes open wide as she grabs it from him, saying, "Hey, this is my jack that disappeared. The blue one. It went missing after we played with Gloria."

I nod and say, "Gloria probably took it. Now it shows up on the porch of the House with a Face. She must've dropped it there. She must live there."

Joella adds, "Gloria was odd from the beginning. She wasn't afraid of finding Lady Llorona in the gully or going to that wedding. Maybe she's the child who disappeared, the one Lady Llorona was searching for."

"Yeah!" Jerred says, teasing. "It's odd that you never knew which house she lived in. Perhaps your odd friend Gloria was Lady Llorona in disguise. Or maybe she is a ghost girl and always lived in that old, haunted house!"

Jenel says, "Are you sure the sign says La Familia Llorones? Do you even know how Llorones is spelled?"

"Not really," Joella replies, "but we could try to find out."

"Are you sure it didn't say La Familia Moralez?" I ask. "That's Gloria's last name."

"I'll go back to the porch and look again and see if the sun face has a blood tear," Jerred offers. "Maybe Rolo will go with me if I tell him what we saw. I can ask him more about Mister Llorón and Lady Llorona to see if he heard about that wedding or knows how to spell their names."

"Geez," Joella says. "I hope you guys will be safe. That house is haunted."

"Let's just take a different route to school," I say, "to avoid that creepy house and forget about Gloria, Lady Llorona, and Mister Llorón. I'm too spooked, hearing about ghosts and seeing strange things. I promise to wear my blue cat-eye glasses from now on."

Jenel agrees and says, "Okay, we won't walk that way unless Jerred and Rolo can figure out who really lives at the House with the Face."

Chapter Thirteen

New Route

Jerred and Joella show us a new route to school toward West Coden Avenue. Jerred shows us a shortcut behind the corner drugstore. We cross an alley and shuffle through a vacant lot with tall weeds in it. Jerred tells us to stay on the dirt trail because skeletons were buried under the weeds. Someone found human bones sticking out of the ground when they were cleaning the lot.

I didn't know which route was worse since there seemed to be scary and haunted places all around our neighborhood. I still have a lot of questions, though. Does the sign really say, La Familia Llorones or did Jerred and Joella read it wrong and it really says La Familia Moralez? Was that the house Gloria had

41

moved to in the neighborhood? If I did see Gloria in that house, was she trapped inside with Lady Llorona and Mister Llorón and was that why she wasn't in school? Why was the sun face crying a blood tear? Or was I seeing things 'cause I didn't have my glasses on? Is the House with a Face really haunted?

Hopefully, Jerred will ask Rolo about what is happening with Lady Llorona and Mister Llorón and their wedding.

...

After school, Joella meets us and says, "Jerred is walking by the House with a Face with Rolo and giving him the scoop about what we saw. He'll let us know what they see. We'll walk the new route home."

Joella, Jenel, and I walk side by side through the lot with weeds where skeletons were found. With every step, I imagine a bony hand coming out of the ground and grabbing my foot. I have my blue cat-eye glasses on to make sure I can see what's there. All of a sudden, Jenel stumbles and falls to the ground in the weeds.

"Ow!" she cries.

Joella and I help her up. "Oh no. Are you okay?" Joella asks as blood runs from Jenel's knee just below her skirt. She helps her pull away the pointy stickers from her knee.

"Yeah, I guess," Jenel says, "but it felt like something tripped me." She moans as she limps and looks back to see what she tripped on.

"Maybe you need to start wearing glasses, too," I say. I look around and don't see anything. "Gee, this lot is scary," I say. "Really scary."

Chapter Fourteen

White Cat

Jerred, Joella, and Jenel pick me up on Thursday morning. We walk up the block to school. "Guess what they saw in the tree at the House with a Face?" Jenel says, sounding excited.

"Gloria?" I guess.

"No," Jenel says, "her white cat Blanca with the red eyes."

"Really?" I say. "Then Gloria has to live there. What about the sign on the porch? And did the sun face still have a red tear?" I ask Jerred.

"We didn't go up to the porch," he says, "so we couldn't see the sign from the sidewalk. But we could see a dark streak under the eye going down the cheek of the sun face. Rolo says he sees that white cat in the gully at night with glowing red eyes. And he also saw a big bobcat with glowing yellow eyes down there chasing the white cat. He says it's either them he hears meowing loudly or it's Lady Llorona and Mister Llorón crying."

"You mean a bobcat with the points on its ears is in the gully now?" I ask, feeling goosebumps on my arms. "Aren't they only in the mountains?"

"That's what I thought," Jerred says. "It seems like the bobcat appeared after we heard that Mister Llorón was seen down there. I have a feeling the white cat is Lady Llorona and the bobcat is Mister Llorón—in disguise."

"See, I did see a red blood tear without my glasses on," I say. "Wow, if that white cat is the Lady Llorona in disguise you guys didn't stare at it, did you?"

"Well," Jerred says, "the white cat was watching us. How strange that it first appeared after we counted 300 stars. We're going back tonight on our bikes to snoop around and see if Gloria or anyone else is around."

Joella tells Jerred, "What if you guys get caught? You might disappear and not make it back home or come back hypnotized in a trance!"

"Then tell Dad or call the police and have them check that house if we don't come back," Jerred replies.

"Did Rolo know how to spell Llorona." I ask, "or did he hear about that wedding?"

"He'll ask his sister Rosa about their wedding," Jerred says, "and how to spell their names."

Jenel says, "It's strange how only Gloria got invited to that wedding and disappeared."

"What's strange is that I saw her in the window," I say. "Then we find the jack she must've taken. And her cat Blanca is hanging around the House with a Face, too. But she's avoiding us for some reason."

We arrive at the corner of 15th Avenue and stop before we cross. A school bus rolls by. When it passes, my friends step off the curb and into the street. Before I follow them, I look at the back of the bus. And I'm stunned by what I see!

Chapter Fifteen

School Bus

"HEY, THERE'S GLORIA!" I shout, pointing at the school bus.

My friends turn, but she's gone. Jenel mocks me and says, "Where? How come only you see her, and we don't? Maybe you're seeing ghosts."

"She was at the back window in that bus," I say. "I saw her and I'm wearing my glasses. She just stared like she was in a trance. She didn't smile or wave."

Jerred and Joella look at each other.

Then Joella says, "Do you mean Gloria was staring like she was hypnotized when she came up the hill from the gully?"

"Yeah," Jenel says, "she tried to fool us that she was under the spell of Lady Llorona after she stared at that bush that started following us. We ran up the hill, but she stayed down there. Then she slowly walked up the hill with her green eyes wide open and never looked at us and just went home. She looked like that family walking in a trance."

"Gloria's eyes were wide open again," I add, "Maybe she's trying to make us think that she's under the spell of Lady Llorona and Mister Llorón after going to that wedding? Or maybe she really is under a spell?"

"She must be going to a Catholic or Jewish school on that bus," Joella says. "Maybe she doesn't want to be your friend anymore. Just forget about her. I'm sure she'll be walking around looking for her white cat again."

"I want to forget her," I say, "but she shows up on every route we take to school. Could she be a ghost haunting the neighborhood or is she just haunting me? Or could she be under a spell and trapped in that House with a Face? That blood tear on the sun face could be like a cry for help!"

"If you really are seeing her," Jenel says, comforting me, "she must be okay if she's on a school bus. At least she isn't trapped in a house all day."

Jerred suggests, "Okay, how about we all go back to the House with the Face with Rolo. Jenel and Darla need to knock and ask for Gloria, since they know her. If she comes to the door and talks, we can see if she's okay or if she acts strange, she may need our help. What do you say? That way you two can read the sign on the porch and look at the sun face."

"I don't know," I say. "I was ready to forget her and not go by that house anymore. What if the Lady Llorona or Mister Llorón answer the door? They could be disguised as real people and put us in a trance! Joella thinks we should forget Gloria, too."

I hope that Jenel agrees with me.

"I don't want to go back," she says. "You guys go by yourselves tonight like you planned and spy on the house."

Chapter Sixteen

Bobcat

After dinner, Jerred rides his three-speed Fastback Sting Ray bike a few blocks over to Rolo's house next to the gully. Rolo's bike is a five-speed with a colorful Mexican serape over the banana seat.

"Look what I used to cover my seat," Rolo says.

"Neato!" Jerred says. "I'll race you up the alley

to spy on that House with the Face. I bet my three-speed is as fast as your five-speed."

Rolo gets there first. They stop behind the House with a Face and look into the yard through the wire fence. The back door is open, but there's no screen door. All of a sudden, they hear loud cries. One is a long and loud yowl that is different than the other.

"Whoa," Jerred says with a moan. "That sounds scary. Is that a cat or a human?"

Rolo says, "That's what I heard in the gully. It could be Lady Llorona or Mister Llorón!"

Jerred shudders and says, "What if they come after us?"

Rolo points and says, "Look, there's yellow eyes in the tree watching us. Maybe it's that bobcat. I'm loading my slingshot with a rock, just in case!"

YEE-OW-RAOW!

The bobcat yowls and jumps off the branch and into the backyard.

"Let's go, it's a big one!" Jerred hollers, turning his bike around.

Rolo looks back to see if the bobcat comes their way. The bobcat is gone, but a man walks into the house. "Wait up, I just saw a man with a long coat and hat go into the house."

"I bet the bobcat is Mister Llorón in disguise," Jerred says. "Remember we saw the white cat in the tree yesterday, with its red eyes? And you said you've seen them both in the gully together, right?"

"Yeah," Rolo says, joking, "the bobcat must be Mr. Bob Llorón and the white cat, Mrs. Blanca Llorona—La Familia Llorones!"

All of a sudden, the white cat prowls and hisses at Rolo from behind the fence. It shows its sharp teeth. Rolo freezes and aims his slingshot at it.

"Yikes, there's Blanca now," he says with a gasp. "We better split. Quit watching Blanca. She might hypnotize you and put you into a trance!"

"I know," Rolo says, "I was looking at her black collar. It had a black heart hanging from it, but I couldn't tell what was on it, something white. Let's come back tomorrow night with Gabriel and Mateo. Their family just moved across the street from me. They're from Mexico, but they go to that Jewish boy's school. They wear those little skull cap beanies on their heads called yarmulkes. They've heard about La Llorona, too. Maybe you can spend the night!"

"Okie dokie," Jerred says. "Gee, I didn't know Jewish people were in Mexico. See you at school." He rides off to his block.

Chapter Seventeen

Porch

On the way to school Friday morning, Jerred tells us what he saw with Rolo at the House with a Face. They plan to go back with two of Rolo's new friends from his block. Jerred insists that we walk by the House with the Face on the way to school. When we get there, he notices something.

"Look, the back door is still open like it was last night," he says. "Rolo saw a man with a long coat and hat walk in there."

"You guys should've asked the man if Gloria was home," I say.

Jenel asks Jerred, "Didn't you describe Mister Llorón as wearing a long coat and a hat?"

"He went in the house too fast," Jerred explains, "but yeah, we think it was him. At first, we heard the bobcat in the tree yowling really loud, but when it jumped down it disappeared. Then the man appeared. We think Mister Llorón is the bobcat. And the white cat, Blanca, that was hissing at Rolo, must've been Lady Llorona. Especially since we saw the cat the night when we counted 300 stars."

"Geez!" Joella shrieks. "Do you think Gloria can disguise herself, too? Maybe she's in disguise as some other cat or maybe she's the sun face that cries blood tears."

"That's why we want to snoop around some more over there," Jerred says, "but we need backup. Rolo and I will walk this way again after school. We'll knock this time to see if anyone comes to the door. You girls should come with us. Maybe Gloria will answer."

I look at the sisters, hoping they'll say no.

Then Jenel asks, "Darla, what do you think? You may see her again, since she keeps appearing to you in windows. Besides I don't want to fall in that ugly lot again."

"I think we should just forget about her like Joella said," I say, "but if you and Joella want to go, I'll go, too!"

...

We walk with Jerred and Rolo to the House with a Face after school. We stop and Jerred asks Jenel to hold his scary story books he checked out from the bookmobile. Jerred says, "Darla, come with us to the porch. We'll knock on the door and you can ask for her if someone answers, since she knows you."

Joella says, "Go ahead, Darla. We'll wait on the side looking at the sun face so we can see that red blood tear stain. And we'll watch the windows, too!"

I take a deep breath and follow Jerred and Rolo to the porch. There's no screen door and the wooden door isn't closed all the way. Jerred's knock pushes it open. He and Rolo look at each other, then into the house.

Jerred says, "Go ahead, Darla, call her."

"Hello?" I say. "Gloria, are you here? Anyone home?" I call out and wait. When no one answers I say, "Okay, I'll be with Jenel and Joella by the sun face."

Rolo whispers, "Jerred, where is that sign you saw that said La Familia Llorones?"

"It was here when the door was closed," he says. "It looks like no one lives here now. I guess they moved and took their sign with them. We don't need to know how to spell the name Llorones now!"

"Should we go in a little ways and see what we find?" Rolo whispers.

"No," Jerred says, "someone could be hiding. Let's wait until tonight when we come back with your friends. Did you ask them to come with us?" he says quietly as floorboards on the porch creak when he takes another step.

"Yeah, Gabriel and Mateo said they'd come," Rolo says, stopping when cries come from inside the house: "Meow... me-ow... yee-oww."

"Did you hear that?" Rolo says. "It sounds like

kittens or a baby crying. Maybe Blanca had kittens from the bobcat."

"Yeah," Jerred says with a chuckle, "maybe they should have left their sign La Familia Llorones since it sounds like a crying family lives here."

"Hurry you guys," Joella says, "what do you see?"

Jenel and I see a red blood streak on the cheek of the sun face. A curtain moves at a window on the second floor, like someone looking out. I grip Jenel's arm and start trembling, "Hey, the curtain on the upper window just moved," I say. "Someone is in there!"

Jenel quivers and says to her sister, "I knew Darla would see someone in the window."

The guys run back to us.

Jerred says, "The house is empty. La Familia Llorones must've moved 'cause their sign with the family name is gone and there's nothing in the house. But we heard kittens meowing that sounded like babies crying."

"Well," I say, "I just saw the curtain move on that top window, so someone is upstairs. You didn't see Blanca or the bobcat?"

"No," Jerred says, "we didn't see the cats that were crying. Maybe they were playing with the curtain upstairs." He grabs Jenel from behind. "Or maybe a ghost. Boo!"

Jenel whimpers and says, "Oo-we! Stop it!

What if the kittens are the kids that Lady Llorona and Mister Llorón hypnotized at their wedding, like Gloria? Maybe they disguise the kids as kittens. The bobcat and Blanca must be upstairs, unless they went to the gully."

We stand looking at the windows of the House with the Face to see if the curtains move again. Even though they don't, it feels like someone is watching from behind them.

Rolo says, "We'll come back tonight with Gabriel and Mateo and snoop around. If we don't see anything, maybe we'll go down the gully, too."

Joella tells Jerred, "I don't think you better come back with the other boys. This house is vacant, so it has to be haunted. It's too scary. You aren't supposed to go to the gully, either!"

"I'm not a 'fraidy cat," he says. "Besides, we've been planning this. Don't tell anyone our plan. We'll figure this mystery out ourselves!"

Chapter Eighteen

Fright Night

On Friday evening, Jerred puts his flashlight and slingshot in a bag and grabs his big boulder marbles. He walks over to Rolo's. They go up the block to pick up Gabriel and Mateo. Their younger sister Miriam answers the door and says that they just left for Rolo's house.

"Wow, how did we miss them?" Rolo asks.

"Maybe they thought they were supposed to meet us at the House with a Face," Jerred says. "Let's walk over there and see if we meet up with them."

"Do you have your flashlight, slingshot, and big marbles?" Rolo says, joking. "Are you ready for a Fright Night?"

"Yeah, let's find a long stick or branch to use as a sword," Jerred says. "Should we take some meat in case we need to throw it at the cats, La Familia Llorones? They might be hungry," he suggests.

"Hmm, that's a good idea," Rolo says, "but then we have to go back to my house. Maybe next time!" Rolo finds a branch on the ground and picks it up.

Jerred and Rolo approach the House with a Face. The front door is still open. They walk around the side to the back to see if Gabriel and Mateo are behind the house. The back door is open, too. There are no cats or brothers anywhere.

"Geez, why didn't they wait for us?" Jerred says. "Maybe they wanted to go in the House with a Face without us. Let's go inside to see if they're snooping around. You lead the way, before it gets any darker."

"Okay, let's see what we find," Rolo says. "But whisper in case someone is upstairs, so they don't hear us. Get your slingshot ready, too. If we don't see anything scary, we can go back in. I'll bring this stick."

The wooden steps creak as they walk up toward the back door. There are big cobwebs at the top and sides of the porch in back. Jerred creeps behind Rolo as they walk into a back room and through a kitchen. They smell something burning.

Rolo spots a lighted candle and matches on the floor in the next room. "Look," he whispers, "a candle is burning. Someone must be here."

"*ME-OW, YEE-OW, Me-ow, Meow.*"

"Oh-oh, the cats," Jerred whispers. "They're upstairs. Let's go up there."

Rolo waves his fingers, motioning to go towards the

stairs. He follows Jerred.

"Shhh, something is ticking," Jerred says. "What if it's a bomb?" he asks nervously as they climb the stairs.

Once at the top, Jerred peeks into a room.

"It's a tick-tock clock on the floor ticking," he says. "Yikes, there's some big black shoes sticking out like someone is lying in the closet—asleep or dead." He jumps back and feels  his heart thumping. "Go peek in the other room where the cats are meowing," Jerred whispers. "If those shoes move, we'll split."

Rolo tiptoes over to the next room to peek at the crying cats. A breeze blows through the window and the door slams shut all of a sudden. Rolo backs away and knocks over empty pop bottles in the hallway. They clang on the floor.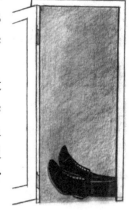

"Run," Rolo blurts out, "that door just slammed shut!" He heads for the stairs and steps on something. He stoops down and grabs a black collar from the floor under his shoe.

An ugly wail cries out: *"YEEE-OOW – YE-OW."*

"It's the bobcat or Mister Llorón!" Jerred shouts

60

and runs down the stairs

Rolo runs behind him to the front door. They look back to make sure no one is coming after them. Then BOOM, Jerred smacks into somebody coming in the door.

"AHHH!" he hollers.

"Hey, we found you guys!" Mateo says, laughing.

Rolo gasps and says, "Whew, glad it's you two! Don't come in here. Someone with big shoes is lying upstairs in the closet. We went for you guys, but you left so we thought you were meeting us here. We think it's Mister Llorón and we don't want to see his skeleton face or yellow eyes. That was scary. I don't want to go back in there again. Then someone slammed the door in the other room, so that could've woken him up. He might grab us. Let's go!"

Gabriel says, "Well, since we're here we can go check and see if we see the same thing."

Jerred says, "We were looking for this girl Gloria and some cats upstairs. We think the cat had kittens, because we heard crying."

"Maybe we'll hear more cries tonight," Rolo says, "if the cats go wandering in the gully. Let's tell my sister Rosa about the House with a Face, the cats, and Gloria, since she seemed to know about Lady Llorona and Mister Llorón's wedding."

Jerred says, "This house is haunted. We don't dare go back in."

"Maybe we better not go in now," Gabriel says to Mateo as they walk behind Rolo and Jerred. "We can come back later and snoop around. Let's go see what his sister says about the strange wedding these guys are talking about."

...

Rolo goes into his house looking for Rosa. His Mom tells him she left to sleep at her classmate's house. Rolo comes back outside and says, "Rosa isn't going to be here tonight. Do you all want to go to the backyard and sneak down to the gully?"

Jerred says, "Let's look for nightcrawlers in the backyard with our flashlights and go to the gully in the morning. It looks too dark, and besides, we might scare the skunks and get sprayed."

"We'll probably hear La Llorona crying again," Gabriel says. "We heard her crying the other night and it was scary, right Mateo?" Gabriel grabs his neck. "Mateo and Miriam got all scared."
Mateo says, "It sounded like she was in the alley close to our house."

"Well, some of us heard her cry," Jerred says,

"but haven't seen her as a ghost. We should count 300 stars and see if she appears tonight. When my sisters and Darla and I did that, a white cat jumped out of the bush in my backyard."

Gabriel looks up at the stars as skinny dragonflies zoom all crazy above their heads. "WATCH OUT," he hollers, "DRAGONFLIES!"

"Cover your mouth with your hands," Mateo says, "they'll sew your lips together!"

"What?" Jerred asks, holding his hands over his mouth. He looks up at the swarm darting back and forth and notices two bats flying above the dragonflies. "Whoa, two bats are swooping all over, too."

Rolo laughs and says, "Where did you hear that dragonflies sew your lips?"

"I heard that when we lived in Mexico," Mateo says. "There are vampire bats there, but they only attack cows and animals."

"What if the bats are Lady Llorona and Mister Llorón in disguise?" Jerred asks.

"Maybe," Rolo says, "if they have red or yellow eyes. But they fly back and forth so fast it's hard to tell. Those brown bats are always out here. So are the dragonflies. They come from the gully. But I'm not afraid of them."

Jerred shines his flashlight on the grass and grabs a nightcrawler. "Check out this huge nightcrawler," he says. "We should go fishing at Coden Lake tomorrow. Do you have a can, Rolo? We can put dirt and grass and catch more."

Rolo goes to the shed and finds an old tin coffee can with a lid. "Look there's more nightcrawlers over here, guys."

Jerred walks slowly over and steps on something that moves and jumps up. "Aahh, I stepped on a snake," he shouts. "There it goes… let's catch it."

Gabriel says, "No, it could be rattlesnake."

Rolo runs and grabs the snake as it curls around, "Not here, these are garter snakes. They eat the night crawlers. They don't bite."

Mateo says, "Wow, can I keep it? We can scare our sister."

Rolo says, "Well, you need something with a lid 'cause it'll climb out. I took one inside in a bucket, but it climbed out and was loose in the house. My mom and Rosa got all mad 'cause they were afraid

to see it or walk in the dark and step on it. We didn't find it for about a week and then we saw it in the window climbing up the screen trying to get out. I was glad we found it. So, I can't bring snakes to the house. They come from the gully."

"Gee, this gully reminds me of Mexico," Gabriel says, joking. "La Llorona is here, too. Thanks for the warning. We'll see what we find to put it in. We better go home now, Mateo, before La Llorona shows up."

Jerred hands them the coffee can with the night crawler in it. "Here, take this for now and see if the snake eats it. You need to make slits in the lid with a knife for air."

"Hasta mañana, amigos. Don't stay out too long," Gabriel says laughing. "La Llorona may show up next." He waves goodbye.

"Your yard is scary," Mateo says, "but fun. ¡Buenas noches!"

"Goodnight. See you tomorrow," Rolo says.

Jerred waves to the brothers. "They're funny guys and they speak good English for being from Mexico. But they look like Jewish boys."

A loud cry comes from the alley. Rolo and Jerred point their flashlights in the alley and see the bobcat pouncing slowly to the gully. The white cat follows and carries a crying kitten by the skin of its neck in her mouth.

"BLANCA," Jerred calls out.

The white cat stops and turns. The bobcat does the same. Jerred and Rolo see two red eyes and a little pair of green eyes and big yellow eyes gleaming at them.

Jerred says, "Look, their glowing eyes are getting bigger. They look like they're coming towards us."

"Well, you called Blanca, so here she comes. SCAT," Rolo hollers. "Blanca doesn't have her collar on because I have it now."

"That's probably what she wants," Jerred whispers, "so throw it back at her or we better run inside. We don't have our slingshots ready."

"Yeah, let's get inside," says Rolo as they walk backwards to the door.

Rolo and Jerred go inside and look out the window, but the cats are gone.

"Strange. They left the House with a Face" Jerred says. "I bet it's Lady Llorona with the same red eyes in disguise. She's holding the baby cat which could've been Gloria since her eyes were green. And Mister Llorón with big yellow eyes. Now they know where you live, Rolo."

Fire

Fire trucks race by on 15th Avenue around 9:00 a.m. Saturday morning. Jenel and Joella ring my doorbell just as the loud sirens stop a few blocks away.

"There must be a fire nearby," Jenel says. "We're following the fire trucks to see where they went. Do you want to go see?"

I ask my mom if I can go to see if there's a fire nearby. She lets me.

Joella says, "We're worried 'cause Jerred is at Rolo's. He lives a few blocks over where the fire trucks might be headed."

Another truck goes by, so we run after it until it stops two blocks away next to the House with a Face. Firemen with hoses blast water into the windows and doors as a crowd gathers along the sidewalk across the street.

We stand by two ladies and overhear them saying that there were two boys running from the house the night before. One lady tells the other that she lives next door and that the house had been vacant; a hobo was staying there until a lady and girl showed up.

Men in uniforms come out of the house with two cages and place them in a van. It looks like a cat or the kittens might be in one of them. The bigger cage may have the bobcat in it. Smoke comes out of the first-floor windows, which are broken. Black water runs over the sun face.

"Look, now the sun face is crying black tears," I point out.

"I wonder if any of the cats died from all the smoke and fire?" Jenel asks.

Joella replies, "Maybe they'll take them to the vet or the Lost Friends League if they're still alive."

"Excuse me," I say to the ladies. "Have they rescued any people from in there?"

"Not yet," one lady replies. "Maybe those stray cats that were always running in and out are in those cages."

"Oh okay," I say, "Did you ever see a girl about our age in that house?"

"No, but the neighbor next door said she saw a lady and a girl there," the lady says. "I did see a girl at the corner getting on a school bus one morning. But I don't know what house she came from. I live across the street."

"Really? Thanks," I say. I turn to Jenel and Joella with a surprised look on my face. "See, I bet it really was Gloria in the window and on the bus."

Joella says softly, "Hmm, unless it was a different girl. We better walk around and see if we find Jerred and Rolo out here, and if not, we better walk to Rolo's to see if they're okay."

Jenel says with a moan, "This is scary, I hope they didn't go into the House with a Face. They could get blamed for the fire. I'm glad that the boys the neighbor saw got out. And that the house didn't burn down."

As we start walking down the block, we see Jerred and Rolo going toward the fire trucks. We tell them there's a fire in the House with a Face. We also heard neighbors saying they saw boys running from the house the night before.

"What?" Jerred asks in shock. "We didn't start any fire, but there was a lit candle on the floor. We didn't run from the house, either. We walked away with Gabriel and Mateo. Maybe they went back later and knocked them over. Or maybe the cats did!"

Rolo explains, "Well, we went inside last night 'cause we thought Gabriel and Mateo were meeting us there when we didn't find them at their house. We saw a lit candle on the floor and heard the cats crying. We went upstairs. A man was lying in the closet. Jerred saw his shoes. The cats were upstairs in another room but when I went to look in, the door slammed shut."

Jerred adds, "Then we heard a loud, ugly cry. It was probably Mister Llorón or the bobcat. We ran downstairs and bumped into Mateo and Gabriel at the door. They wanted to go back in but said they might wait until later."

"And look what I found upstairs in the hallway,"

Rolo lifts up his hand holding something black. "The collar that I saw on Blanca the night she hissed at me. It's a white cat in a black heart! We were in my backyard last night and saw the bobcat and Blanca carrying a kitten to the gully. Jerred hollered 'Blanca' and they stopped and stared at us with glowing red, green, and yellow eyes all growing bigger. We thought they might come towards us, so we went inside."

I grab the collar Rolo says he found. "Oh my gosh… it's Gloria's choker! She has been in the house. I wonder why she left it there. She was always wearing it. It was her mom's, but then Rolo saw Blanca wearing it. That's strange, especially if you think that Blanca is Lady Llorona. Then could her mom be Lady Llorona? We met Gloria before she went to that wedding, though…"

Joella says, "Well, Lady Llorona is probably her mom now."

"This is giving me the creeps," Jenel says quivering. "What if Gloria is Lady Llorona disguised as a girl? It seems like the night Jerred and Joella counted the 300 stars, the white cat appeared. Next Gloria appears in our neighborhood and then disappears. We never saw Gloria with Blanca, either. Then Mister Llorón and a bobcat appear in our neighborhood. See, you called their spirits here from New Mexico by counting to 300 stars!"

Jerred says, "Not sure, but, we had already heard Lady Llorona was in the gully here in Denver before we counted the stars. And if you were with

Gloria and you saw Lady Llorona in disguise, then she can't be disguised twice."

"Well, real people may have been staying in the House with a Face," I add, "I heard the neighbors say that a hobo was staying there for a few weeks and also a lady with a girl. One neighbor saw a girl getting on a school bus one morning. Gloria and her parents may have been staying there. If the house is supposed to be haunted, the ghosts could have scared them away. Or maybe after the wedding, Lady Llorona and Mister Llorón followed them to this house. Anyway, can I keep the choker? Maybe we'll meet up with Gloria again and I can give it to her!"

Jenel asks, "What's a hobo?"

Joella responds, "A man who doesn't have a job, home, or car and wanders around staying in different places."

"Unless…" I say, "the hobo was Gloria's dad and that's where she was staying with her mom and Blanca. That's kind of sad if this wasn't her real home. The real owner came and probably made them leave. That explains why she disappeared," I say.

"Maybe the bus took her to a boarding school and that's why she didn't return," Joella says. "I don't know. This sure is a big mystery."

"What's a boarding school?" Jenel asks.

"It's a school that allows students to sleep there

and stay for the week or the whole school year," Joella explains.

"Only people with money send their kids to boarding schools," Rolo says. "Besides why would Lady Llorona and Mister Llorón get rid of their child again?"

"I think it was Mister Llorón who the lady thinks is a hobo," Jerred says. "He disappeared by disguising himself as the bobcat. They were all in disguise as real people or cats. The fire might have started last night and that's why they ran to the creek."

"Well, we saw two cages being taken out," Jenel says. "There were cats inside, but we don't know if they were still alive or if it was Blanca. Then maybe Lady Llorona and Mister Llorón are captured, if the cats were still alive or dead."

"Maybe there were other stray cats in the house," I say, "since you guys heard kittens crying or maybe they went back to the house after the gully last night."

"If it was the bobcat," Jerred says, "he will probably get taken to the mountains and released. Then Lady Llorona and Mister Llorón will be separated again. That's kind of sad. But at least we don't have to worry about any of them anymore!"

"I wouldn't count on that," Rolo says with a smirk. "They'll return to the gully. They always do. They are spirits, remember!"

Chapter Twenty

No Trespassing

Two big firemen walk up to us all of a sudden.

"Hello, boys," one of them says. "A neighbor across the street says she saw you two come out of that house last night. Can we ask you a few questions separately?"

Jerred says, "Uh... okay."

"Sure," Rolo says, "but we didn't start no fire."

One fireman takes Jerred to his truck while the other takes Rolo to another one.

"Oh no," Joella says. "I hope they don't get arrested."

I say, "I wonder if they'll tell them about Lady Llorona and Mister Llorón or about Gloria disappearing."

Jenel says, "Well, how come they just didn't start asking them questions here. They need to find that hobo and ask him."

After about fifteen minutes, Jerred shakes the fireman's hand. He comes back to us. Rolo talks to the other fireman and points down the block.

"What did he ask and what did you say?" Joella asks.

"Are you in trouble Jerred?" Jenel says. "Is he

going to let our parents know?"

Jerred says, "Boy, was I ever scared. He asked for my full name, address, phone number, and age. Then he wanted to know why we went into a vacant house and if we knew it was trespassing. I said we thought it was the house of a girl named Gloria, since her white cat was there and maybe she was there, too. Because Darla thought she saw her in the window a few days before. So, we went in and saw a lit candle in one room and heard a clock ticking upstairs and saw a man's big shoes in the closet. Then we heard cats crying in another room but when we went to look the door slammed shut and we got scared and left."

"What did the fireman say?" I said. "Did you tell him Gloria disappeared?"

Jerred explains, "He was writing it all down. No, I didn't say she disappeared. Maybe I should have. Then he asked if there were other boys with us. So, I told him two other boys that Rolo knows got there as we were leaving but they didn't go in because we told them someone was in there. Then he said it's dangerous to go into vacant homes, that they're supposed to be locked up. So he said the neighbors saw the doors were always open. We didn't break in, so we aren't in trouble. But he's going to call my parents and keep my name. He warned if I am ever caught going into a vacant home again, I may get into trouble, especially if it's a house that catches fire. He said the neighbors mentioned seeing a hobo that was staying there, so they want to question him, too."

"Wow," I ask, "Did you mention that Mister Llorón could've been the hobo? Or mention Lady Llorona?"

"No, I wonder if Rolo did," Jerred says. He looks over as Rolo walks back. "What did you tell him?" Jerred asks him.

"I told him I heard the house was haunted and we went inside to see if there were ghosts," Rolo says. "And we saw a candle burning and cats were crying upstairs, and something was ticking. So, we went up to look and there were shoes in the closet. Then someone slammed the other door shut. So, we got scared and left. Then we ran into Gabriel and Mateo at the door. They said they might come back. But I told the fireman I didn't think they did since we found a snake and they went home happy. He asked me my name, address, and phone number and said he would let my parents know that I was in a vacant house that caught on fire. Then he said we can't be trespassing on other people's property, that it's against the law. He also said that nobody knows what happened to the owner of the House with a Face. The fireman wants to talk to Gabriel and Mateo, so I told him where they live. What did you say, Jerred?"

"About the same thing," he says, "but not that it was haunted. I said we thought a girl named Gloria lived there. But I didn't say anything about La Familia Llorones. Glad you didn't either! How strange about the owner. I wonder what our parents will do?"

...

I walk to school with Jenel, Joella, and Jerred Monday morning. Jerred says the fireman called his parents. He is not allowed to go into vacant houses again because the hobo could have grabbed them and locked them inside. We'll find out at school if Rolo got in any trouble. We walk by the House with a Face to see what damage was done.

Jenel points at the sun face. "Oh no, the poor sun face is covered with black ash streaks, and some red streaks too, like she's crying blood again. The first-floor windows and doors are boarded up. And look, there's a box on the back porch. Let's go see what's in it!"

Joella says, "No, we aren't supposed to be going onto this property anymore. Why don't you go see what's in it, Darla?"

"Just me by myself?" I ask. "Okay!" I take a deep breath and creep over. I look inside the box. It's stuffed with pop bottles, a tick-tock clock, and a metal picture frame with lines of little beads.

"Wow, these things didn't burn up," I say as I pull them out to show them. I turn the picture frame over; staring back at me are a scary, crying skeleton lady with red eyes and a white veil over her face, a man with a hat and half-skeleton face with yellow eyes. All their teeth are showing like they're smiling. They're dressed in wedding clothes and she's wearing the choker with the white cat that Rolo found.

"Yikes, how scary!" I say with a shiver, "They're the newlyweds, Mrs. Lady Llorona and Mr. Llorón!" I hold up the picture frame and run to show them.

"Oo-weee!" Jenel shouts, "They really exist and did get married. Now we know what they looked like. I wonder who took the picture?"

"Probably Gloria," I say. "She went to the wedding.

I want to keep this and show it to my cousins in New Mexico and tell them about La Llorona and Mister Llorón in Colorado."

Jerred warns, "Just don't stare at it too long. It might hypnotize you. But let's show it to Rolo first, since he told us about their wedding. They even look how his sister described them."

"Wow, they really do," Joella says and points to a sign in a window. "Look at what that sign says: NO TRESPASSING. Nobody better go inside now."

As we walk away, I look back at the top windows, which aren't boarded up. The curtains move in one of them. I look at my friends and say, "Hey, I just saw the curtains move. Could Gloria still be in there?"

"Again?" Jenel and Joella say at the same time.

"I really did," I say. "Wait!"

I run up to the front porch where I see another NO TRESPASSING sign on the door. I hang the black choker with the white cat on the doorknob, just in case Gloria, her Mom, Blanca, or La Familia Llorones return.

About the Author-

Karen D. Gonzales loves hearing stories about La Llorona, so she decided to write this story inspired by childhood memories. She enjoys attending cultural events, genealogy research, reading, writing and volunteering. She is Coordinator of the Denver Las Comadres and Friends National Latino Book Club. Karen has a cat, a son, three grandkids and both her parents lived to be centenarians.

The Mystery of La Llorona and Mister Llorón won 2nd Place in the Sandra Seaton Michel Middle School Story 2022 Biennial Competition in Letters with the National League of American Pen Women.

About the Illustrator-

Dolores Guerrero is an American artist, she is known for her contemporary art through paintings, murals, and graphic art. Her art reflects her advocacy towards the empowerment movement for the Chicano and Latin community. She resides in Los Angeles.

Made in United States
Troutdale, OR
11/22/2023

14836669R00050